Jungle nama

Also by Amitav Ghosh

The Glass Palace

The Hungry Tide

The Living Mountain: A Fable for Our Times

Mahaparbat: Ek Kahani Hamare Daur Ki

Smoke and Ashes: A Writer's Journey Through Opium's Hidden Histories

Jungle Nama

a Story of the Sundarban

Retold by **Amitav Ghosh**

illuminated by **Salman Toor**

FOURTH ESTATE • *New Delhi*

First published in India in hardback by Fourth Estate 2021
An imprint of HarperCollins *Publishers*

4th Floor, Tower A, Building No. 10, DLF Cyber City,
DLF Phase II, Gurugram, Haryana -122002
www.harpercollins.co.in

This edition published in India by Fourth Estate 2024

2 4 6 8 10 9 7 5 3 1

P-ISBN: 9789362133854
E-ISBN: 9789353579135

Book design by Bonita Vaz-Shimray
Typeset in Adobe Jenson Pro
Printed and bound at
Thomson Press (India) Ltd

MIX
Paper | Supporting responsible forestry
FSC® C010615

This book is produced from independently certified FSC® paper
to ensure responsible forest management.

For Annu Jalais

Many great rivers rise in the Himalaya
the Ganga among them, and the Brahmaputra.
Flowing down from west and east, they meet in Bengal,
and branch into numberless streams, some vast, some small.
Still they multiply, courses splitting as they flow,
creating a tangled, green archipelago.
Thousands of islands rise from the rivers' rich silts,
crowned with forests of mangrove, rising on stilts.
This is the Sundarban, where laden waters give birth;
to a vast jungle that joins Ocean and Earth.

I

This realm was once under the sway of Dokkhin Rai;
a mighty spirit feared by all under the sky.
He preyed on humans, in a tiger avatar;
whomever he wanted he'd take for his shikar.
Under his rule all beings shivered in terror;
day after day, they looked heavenwards in prayer.
At length their entreaties crossed the Empty Quarter;
from Araby there came two beings of great power.
One was the Mistress of the Forest, Bon Bibi;
the other was her brother, Shah Jongoli.
Bon Bibi was strong, but full of compassion;
her brother was a warrior, his powers were legion.

The strangers' arrival didn't elude Dokkhin Rai;
nothing in his realm escaped his unblinking eye.
'Who are these two?' he thought. 'Why're they in my forest?
Just look at them, ever so calm and self-possessed.

Do they think they can enter without permission?
It seems that this pair is asking for a lesson.’

Instantly he dispatched a ghostly army,
thinking they’d soon dispose of this trifling enemy.
But no sooner did the spirits spring to attack,
than they screeched in fright and came flying swiftly back.
‘They’re too strong,’ they wailed, ‘this is a fearsome pair!’
‘You cowards!’ roared Dokkhin Rai. ‘You’re easy to scare.
It’s up to me now, I’ll deal with them on my own.
Get out of my way, you fools, I’ll fight them alone.’

At once Dokkhin Rai assumed his tiger disguise;
trusting that the mere sight would sear the strangers' eyes;
they'd take to their heels, they'd never give battle;
not for a moment did he think they'd test his mettle.

But fight they did, defying his earth-shaking roars;
nor did they flinch from his fearsome, flesh-tearing claws.
Every blow he struck they answered with many more;
they pinioned his limbs and bound his taloned forepaws.
Spasms of pain shot through him, sharpening as he fought;
he flailed with all his strength, but the bindings held taut.

The tiger's stripes, which had danced like the flames of a fire,
now fell still, the embers of a fading pyre.
Lying prostrate, pinned under Shah Jongoli's thigh,
what could Dokkhin Rai think but that his end was nigh?

But he was wrong—to finish him wasn't their mission,
    they had come there with a different intention.
What they wanted to end was his tyranny,
    this they did by confining him to a boundary.
They drew a line, to mark a just separation,
    between the forest, and the realm of the human.
To Dokkhin Rai was given the jungles of the south,
    where land and water mingle, at the rivers' mouth.
No human would come there, nor could he go outside,
    he would live a life of plenty, reigning with pride.

Thus did Bon Bibi create a dispensation,
    that brought peace to the beings of the Sundarban;
every creature had a place, every want was met,
    all needs were balanced, like the lines of a couplet.

II

But in this fleeting world, nothing is forever,
desire is potent, and greed hard to conquer.
The sprouting of avarice begins in the spring,
when bees are busy and flowers are blossoming.

So it was for Dhona, renowned as the Rich One;
sadly his wealth had not brought him satisfaction.
He had prospered in trade, with Mona, his brother,
who was a man of a quite different temper.
Content at home, Mona liked his comfort and peace;
he'd worked long and hard, and was glad of his release.
Dhona, on the other hand, always wanted more;
not for him a life of quiet contentment ashore.

There's much to be had there, I'll take all I can see
Honey, wax and timber, and all of it for free!

That spring Dhona was seized by an aching desire;
    'I'll go to the mangroves, seven ships will I hire.
There's much to be had there, I'll take all I can see;
    honey, wax and timber, and all of it for free!'

To his brother he said: 'Now listen to me, bhai:
    I've got an idea about something we should try.
I think it's high time we took on a daring venture;
    we'll make a great fortune, our biggest ever.
It's springtime now and the mangroves are filled with hives.
    Let's try to collect the richest hoard of our lives.
Instead of taking one ship, let's go with seven.
    We should seize all we can and come home brim-laden.'

Listening to this, Mona's heart filled with misgiving.
    'Bhai,' he said, 'this is beyond my understanding.
Don't we have enough? Why another cargo?
    What we've got already will last a lifetime and more.
Those who enter the forest should go out of need,
    or they'll court danger; tigers know the smell of greed.

Why are you so acquisitive, what do you lack?
Take what you want from me, no need to give it back.
We own so much already; why the disappointment?
Life's most splendid gift is that of contentment.'

Brusquely Dhona brushed his brother's advice aside.
'A dull life is something I never could abide.
Grief comes to those who dawdle, idle and well fed.
Their fortunes waste away while they lie home abed.
Where does it say that it's wrong to be venturesome?
Is it greedy to want to add to your income?
Please join me brother, you're someone I can trust;
I want you along, though I'll go alone if I must.'

The Rich One would not listen, that was all too clear.
'Forgive me, bhai,' said Mona, 'but I'm staying here.

Still, as much as I can, I'll try to help you;
        I'll find you seven vessels and for each one a crew.
You'll need many sailors for such a big fleet;
        to hire so many lascars will be no easy feat.
Every ship will need a serang and a tindal,
        to be properly manned, from agil to peechhil.
But you can leave it all to me, I'll do my part;
        to find what you need I'll scour every river-ghat.'

Mona signed on many men, going from port to port;
        but at the end of his search he was still one man short.
Back to Dhona he went, to say: 'Listen, bhai.
        I've found the ships, but of lascars we're still a man shy.
I looked everywhere but could not fill the roster;
        without another man your fleet won't pass muster.'

Said Dhona: 'I know a boy who'll get the job done.
        Remember that cousin of ours, the poor, sad one?
He'll take any job, he cannot afford to choose;
        at no cost to speak of, I'll put him to good use.'

III

The boy Dhona had in mind was a poor relation,
who lived with his mother, in great deprivation.
So miserable was this fellow, so rarely glad,
that people called him Dukhey, which means 'the Sad-Lad'.

To the hut of this lad, Dhona now made his way.
Standing outside, he called out: 'Dukhey! Dukhey!'

'Salaam,' came the answer. 'Is that you there, chacha?'
'Yes, it's me, come out. I'm here to see how you are.'

Dukhey, stepping out, salaamed his uncle anew.
'Welcome to our humble home. Is all well with you?'

'I'm glad to see you,' said Dhona. 'As for me, I'm fine.
I had a dream last night; it felt like a sign.

I saw your late father, lying on his deathbed.
        "Dhona," he said, "I lay Dukhey's care on your head."
I told him I'd serve him like a faithful khidmatgar;
        that's why I've come here now, to see how you are.'

'My dear chacha,' said Dukhey, 'that's too kind of you;
        it has been so long, we wondered whether you knew:
We've fallen on hard times, I earn very little.
        I couldn't find any work but as a herder of cattle.
My wages I give to my mother, just a few pice;
        with that we get by, on a little daal and rice.'

Dhona replied, feigning shock: 'Why, what a shame!
        A grown boy! Cattle-herding isn't good for your name.
Why not come with me and learn to be a sailor?
        You can see the whole world working as a lascar.
I've outfitted a fleet, for the tideland jungle.
        You'll learn a new trade, and the arts of survival.
You'll be making good money even as you learn;
        your Ma'll be happy, she'll be glad to see you earn.

And when we're back I'll arrange a wedding for you.
I'll find you a wife who's pretty and well-to-do.'
Taking out some coins Dhona put them in the boy's hand.
'They're for your mother, they'll help her understand.'

The mention of marriage had made the boy's heart leap.
He took the coins to his mother: 'They're for you to keep.
Chachaji says it's a shame to be a cowherd;
he'll teach me to sail, he's given me his word.
He's put together a fleet, for a long voyage.
This money's an advance, to secure my passage.
He's going to the tideland jungle, he wants me in his crew,
he's promised to pay me well, give me my due.
And when we're back he'll even arrange my wedding.
Poor as I am, what could be a greater blessing?'

Though old and frail, Dukhey's mother had more wisdom,
than can be found in many a revered ashram.
She knew her son was guileless, wedded to truth,
easily exploited, in the restlessness of youth.

The Mangroves are home to predators of every kind
Some you'll never see, but they will enter your mind

'Listen, Dukhey,' she said, 'I want the best for you.
Take care with Dhona, you don't know him like I do.
He'll make big promises, tempt you with money;
you know little of the world, and of men's villainy.
The tideland forest is a realm of great danger,
few men know it well, it's no place for a stranger.
The mangroves are home to predators of every kind,
some you'll never see, but they will enter your mind.
I can't lose you, Dukhey, you are my only son;
I have nobody else, no other child, just one.
Dhona's greed exceeds his wit; why join that man's fleet?
We're not dying of hunger, we have enough to eat.
I want you to be safe; riches I don't need.
Why sail abroad now? With no family yet to feed?'

'But,' said Dukhey, 'going abroad's what everyone does.
With boys of my age, it's what we always discuss.
I'm of the right age now, what will happen later?
Is it my fate to be destitute forever?

If sailing abroad is ordained by my kismet,
I must do it at once, or else that door will shut.'

The old lady saw that she was getting nowhere.
'Send Dhona to me; let him speak to me foursquare.'

The boy left and sent his uncle alone inside.
'Bhabhiji, salaam,' he said, to which she replied:
'You've turned my son's mind; he wants to sail abroad.
Whatever it was that you said, it's struck a chord.
But what's to become of me? A solitary widow?
What if I lose him? It would be a death blow.'

'I swear,' said the Rich One, 'your worries are groundless.
He'll be like a son to me, that I promise.
And this too I swear, after I bring him back;
I'll give him a lavish wedding, there's nothing he'll lack.'

On hearing Dhona's pledge the old lady gave in;
grasping his fingers, she said: 'I trust you, you're kin.
I'm giving you charge of my boy, my only child.
Take good care of him, specially out in the wild.'

'I swear to you,' said Dhona, 'I'll look after him.
Please rest easy, you will have him back in good trim.'

Forlornly the old woman helped Dukhey prepare.
When he'd finished she whispered: 'Oh my son, beware.
You're going to the tideland where dangers are legion.
In the mangrove forest many strange things happen.
It's the land of Dokkhin Rai, a hungry shape-shifter;
he hunts humans, in the form of a tiger.
Unearthly beings of all sorts flock to his durbar;
for the spirits of the wild, he's a great sirdar.
He talks like a pishach, in an inhuman tongue,
when he speaks you won't know from where his voice has sprung.

He loves to prey on souls that are meek and humble;
a good lad like you he'll find irresistible.
It's not just flesh he craves, he likes to kindle greed;
to wake the demon in man is his greatest need.
He won't just snatch you, he'll wait for a betrayal;
whetting avarice, he can set men's heads awhirl.
If he comes after you, stand your own ground, don't run;
every demon, remember, has an ichneumon.
Don't panic, don't get your head in a chukker;
there's someone you can turn to when in need of succour.
She's the Lady of the Jungle, Ma Bon Bibi;
she'll protect you, with her brother Shah Jongoli.
But when you call Bon Bibi, you must do it right,
or your words won't carry, you must help them take flight.
Be sure to cast your call in dwipodi-poyar,
it'll give your voice wings, it's the meter of wonder;

its cadence will strengthen your words; they'll gain in power;
it'll work its magic by tying your thoughts together;
into couplets of twenty-four syllables,
that sometimes rhyme, and sometimes use half-
rhymed vocables.
Compose them well, and your lines will reach Bon Bibi,
if there's enough faith in your heart, she'll come, you'll see.'

Now with a farewell salaam, Dukhey got up to leave;
and so he went his way, leaving her to grieve.

IV

Meanwhile Mona'd been busy, readying the fleet,
making sure it was well-stocked, all ship-shape and neat.
By the time Dhona and Dukhey arrived at the ghat,
the decks were all scrubbed, with the oars stacked athwart.
It took Dukhey no time to learn to row and climb rope;
for once he was cheerful, his heart full of hope.

Then came the day for the fleet to weigh anchor;
ranks of oars flashed as Dhona shouted out the order.
A short way downriver they passed Bakon Hati;
then came Santoshpur in the same territory.
The sun had almost set when they approached the shore;
they moored the ships tight and put away every oar.
At dawn the next day, when Dhona gave the command;
they lowered their shoulders and pulled away from land.

Now with a farewell salaam, Dukhey got up to leave;
and so he went his way, leaving her to grieve

Now they came to a great labyrinth of water;
oars flashing, they crossed many a mighty river.

One night at Phool Ali they anchored with the tide;
early next morning they crossed to the other side.
Nearby were mangroves, knotted in a dense tangle;
hopes rising, Dhona led them into the jungle.
But it was all in vain, the forest was barren;
Dhona came back dejected, his spirits shaken.
He decided now to move on to Gaurkhali;
after the ships had moored he called an assembly.
'We'll stay here tonight,' he said, 'no need to go further;
tomorrow let's see, maybe we'll do better.'

Next day Dhona picked who'd go with him to explore.
To his chosen men he said: 'Come, let's go ashore.
But not you, Dukhey, you stay on board and beware!
If you step ashore you'll be in trouble, I swear.'

They entered the forest, Dhona leading the way;
    but the woods were so thick that they soon went astray.
The jungle was dense, at times almost impassable;
    in the murky gloom nothing was discernible.

Blindly they crossed the invisible boundary,
    that marked the edge of Dokkhin Rai's territory.
In this realm the shape-shifter was the reigning numen;
    nothing escaped him, his eyes were not human.
He saw them the moment they crossed into his land;
    'Who're these men?' he thought. 'Why've they come here
    in a band?
Look how they're lumbering about, clumsy and noisome.
    What can they be here for but to raid my kingdom?
If their intention was not to loot and maraud,
    they wouldn't think of coming here, in such a large horde.
I'd almost forgotten that sharp human odour,
    the taste of their blood, and the tang of their liver.
They haven't asked my leave nor made an offering;
    they want the forest's wealth, in exchange for nothing.

In this realm the shape-shifter was the reigning numen,
Nothing escaped him, his eyes weren't human

To enter the jungle without my permission,
is to ask to be taught a suitable lesson.
As trespassers they're fair game, it's my lucky chance;
I'll go to Gaurkhali and lead them on a dance.'

So the jungle lord spun a web of illusion;
conjuring up visions, laden with temptation.
With consummate ease he made honeycombs appear.
'Look! Hives!' cried Dhona. 'Like answers to a prayer.'
But the first hive he opened held a strange surprise.
There was nothing in the comb! No honey, no prize.
So with the others, they were all empty within;
Dhona gaped in disbelief, burning with chagrin.

'What's this devilry?' thought Dhona. 'Where's the honey?
Some being is playing tricks, someone unearthly.
My eyes show me honeycombs, filled with riches;
but when I touch them nothing comes into my clutches.'

So it went on, all through that day and many more;
great riches would appear but only to withdraw.
'Am I cursed or is it some demonic plot?'
Finding no answer, Dhona thought of one last resort.
'It could be that I need to find out in a dream,
whether these tricks are a part of some devilish scheme.'

Flummoxed and fearful, he lay down and shut his eyes;
and soon, in his sleep, he saw a strange shape arise;
a visage so fearsome that his blood ran cold.
Shivering in fright he thought: 'What's this I behold?'
Still sleeping he murmured aloud: 'Who are you, sir?
Identify yourself, I must know who you are.'

Then he became aware of a voice in his head,
not speaking in words, but planting thoughts in their stead.
'You want to know who I am? Then listen to me:
the one who owns this forest, know that I am he.
My father was a deva, Dondobokkho;
he ruled the forests of this great archipelago.

These islands are my kingdom, I am Dokkhin Rai;
I am the one who rules under this southern sky.
You've come here like dacoits, without asking my leave;
you can't fool me, I know you've come to steal and thieve.
Did you think you could rob me without my knowing?
Whoever you are, you're in for a reckoning.'

'My name is Dhona,' the Rich One whispered in his dream.
'By coming here I meant you no disesteem.
Was it you who played these cruel tricks on my eyes?
Showing me wealth and then cheating me of the prize?'

Dokkhin Rai laughed, and Dhona trembled in his sleep.
'Those who'd take from me must give me something to keep.
Not until you promise an offering of value,
will there be a smidgeon of honey for you.'

Turning over, Dhona murmured: 'But my lord!
What can I give you? I've nothing of value on board.'

'You're wrong there, Dhona,' said Dokkhin Rai with a laugh.
'I have no need for gold coins, or that kind of stuff.
What I love best is the taste of human blood;
there's no scarcer thing in this realm of mangroves and mud.
There was a time once when I hunted far and wide;
then came some rude strangers and confined me inside.
Unable to leave, I've long had to nurture my thirst;
but you've solved my problem by coming here first.
All you need do is give up a chosen victim;
I'll fill your ships with goods if I can but have him.'

When the meaning of these words dawned on Dhona,
he recoiled in his sleep, his insides aflutter.
'My sailors have wives and children to go back to.
How can I surrender any of them to you?'

Dokkhin Rai replied: 'I don't want a family man;
for you, I'll make it as easy as I can.
I'll make do with a disposable young fellow;
I'll pick out some sorry wretch, scrawny and callow.

And I've seen just the right one, that lad over there.
You need only sail off, leaving him in my lair.'

'Dukhey?' cried Dhona, and the sound went to the boy's ear.
He woke with a start: 'Is that my name I hear?'

Meanwhile Dokkhin Rai was still inside Dhona's mind:
'You heard right—Dukhey's the one you must leave behind.'

'Please, not him,' said Dhona. 'I've sworn to keep him safe.
His mother's a poor widow; she'll die without her waif.
I'll leave this forest. Your demand is excessive.
I'll take my men back. A life is too much to give.'

'What? You think you can just run away?' roared Dokkhin Rai.
'I'll sink your entire fleet if you even try.
You and your men will feed many a crocodile;
don't you dare think of escape—Dhona, it's futile.
You were caught in my coils when you entered this raj;
you owe a debt to the crown and mine is the taj.'

Still sleeping, Dhona trembled at Dokkhin Rai's threat.
'Tell me, Lord,' he begged. 'How can I work off this debt?'

'You know already. Your dues are easy to defray.
When you go, just leave behind that lad, Dukhey.'

'But why,' said Dhona, 'is he the one you've chosen?
He's just a sad wretch, fatherless and forsaken.
If your thirst for human blood is so very strong;
then take me—it was I who brought these men along.'

'I don't want you, or any leathery lascar;
it's the boy I want, all innocent and tender.'

Dokkhin Rai's words made Dhona sink into despair;
try as he might, he saw no way out of the snare.
At last he gave in, saying: 'What must I do?
Tell me how you want Dukhey to be handed to you.'

Dokkhin Rai guffawed. 'Dhona, you're wise to agree.
    Your first step should be to sail to Kedokhali.
That's where the boy must be left, it's my favoured haunt.
    It's there too that you'll get all the wealth that you want.'

Some of Dhona's murmurs had carried to Dukhey;
    he began to wonder if some game was at play.
'Is chacha in league with some inhuman power?
    Some demonic force that wants me handed over?
Could it be Dokkhin Rai, as my mother said?
    If it really is he then I might as well be dead.
Uncle Dhona will go home laden with riches,
    leaving me behind to pay a demon's wages.
He'll act pious and kindly, like some grand emir,
    giving alms to every sadhu, pir and fakir.
When people ask what happened to poor young Dukhey,
    he'll say: "A tiger got him while we were away."
Only Ma will mourn me, she'll cry herself blind.
    Hasn't she suffered enough? Fate is so unkind!'

V

Next morning, Dhona set course for Kedokhali;
watching from afar, Dokkhin Rai chortled in glee.
'Dhona's going where I told him to, that's a good sign.
Since he's keeping his bargain, now I must keep mine.'
It took him but an instant to cross the jungle;
like lightning word spread of the master's arrival.
The bees came swarming to him, they numbered in lakhs:
he ordered them all to yield their honey and wax.
Quickly they went to work, filling thousands of hives;
the swarms laboured harder than ever in their lives.

Dhona exulted as his ship approached the shore,
as though he had already pocketed a crore.
Entering the jungle he found a grand display;
there were hives everywhere, a bountiful array.
Quickly he made sure that it was no illusion;
the hives were all brimming, in perfect condition.

Having gloated over his soon-to-be hoard;
          Dhona ordered a feast and then fell asleep on board.
Soon, in his dreams there appeared again that visage;
          Dokkhin Rai had returned, to reaffirm his pledge.

'You see now, Dhona, what's in my power to grant?
          Tomorrow in the jungle, you'll get what you want.
At a sign from me the bees will carry their combs,
          straight to your vessels for you to take to your homes.
Then, my good fellow, it will come time for our tryst;
          you will have to make good your debt to the forest.
Do not forget the bargain we've made on Dukhey,
          your pledge must be fulfilled without any delay.
Beware! I want to hear no excuse or pretext—
          or it's your life that will be in jeopardy next.'

With these words the deva vanished into the night,
          while Dhona slept on, till the first crack of daylight.

Only after the men had eaten their repast,
did he tell them: 'This day will not be like the last.
In the jungle today, we mustn't lift a finger;
our work will be done without our having to stir.
Every one of you must carry a blindfold;
and you must make sure to tie it whenever you're told.
When it's all finished, you can look on and admire;
but you can't ask questions, or your fate will be dire.'

With these words, Dhona led his men to the jungle,
where at once they sensed something inexplicable;
An uncanny feeling, a bristling in the air,
a sensation that caused a prickling in the hair.
All at once the leaves began to move and tremble,
as if shaken by a force, potent yet spectral;
they could feel a presence, gathering like a cloud,
unseen yet active, like an invisible crowd.

At Dhona's word, every man tied on his blindfold.
'Don't you dare peep, or you'll be up on a scaffold!'

Unseen, yet active,

Like an invisible crowd

Dukhey, like the others, did as Dhona said;
he hugged his trembling knees, as wild thoughts
whirled through his head.
All around them now, there arose a busy hum;
the air began to throb, like the skin of a drum.
Seized with dread, the men huddled together in fear;
none could make sense of the uncanny atmosphere.

An age seemed to pass before Dhona spoke again:
'I must check the ships; stay as you are until then.'
Leaving the men Dhona headed for the river;
and again spoke that voice, setting his head astir:
'Look into the holds of your ships; see what I've wrought;
see what a honey'd treasure Dukhey's life has bought.'

Dhona looked in the holds, and with his own eyes he saw,
that they were all full and couldn't take any more.
Dokkhin Rai laughed, seeing Dhona's amazement.
'This is nothing, I'll give you a still better present.

The value of wax is greater than that of honey;
        that's what I'll give you, you'll make much more money.
A deal like ours deserves the finest reward,
        take my offer, let the honey be dumped overboard.'

Dhona, ever-avaricious, leapt at this offer;
        soon the bees returned, on Dokkhin Rai's order.
Now again the jungle began to buzz and hum;
        the air was filled once more with an unearthly scrum.
In a trice the holds were emptied by the buzzing horde;
        then they were filled again, with a waxen hoard.

'It's done,' said Dokkhin Rai, 'you've got your trove of wax;
        but for a fortune like this you must pay a tax.
Tomorrow is when you must settle your debt;
        or you'll learn that I'm not one to make an idle threat.'

'It'll be done,' said Dhona, 'please have no doubt on that score;
        I'll find some way of bringing Dukhey ashore.

He suspects nothing, he will do what I say;
        he and I'll stay behind when the others go away.'

'Good,' said Dokkhin Rai. 'Call your men, let them marvel;
        let them feast their eyes on this wondrous spectacle.'

'Come lascars!' shouted Dhona. 'Take your blinds off now.
        The job's done, you'll see, but you will never know how.'

When the men saw the wax there rose a great uproar.
        'Who loaded the boats while we were all ashore?
Was it a rakshas or jinn? Pishach or afreet?
        It's best to be gone before they scupper the fleet.'

The men begged Dhona: 'Let's leave now, our work is done.'
        But he wouldn't listen: 'No! We must wait for the sun.'

Of all the sailors, none was more troubled than Dukhey;
        he lay awake all night, dreading the next day.

VI

At dawn Dhona announced: 'It's come time to depart.
Men, take six of our ships and make an early start.
I will come in the seventh, alone with Dukhey.
That way he'll learn more, I've much to teach him today.'

On hearing these words a tremor went through the boy;
'Why just me?' he thought. 'This must be some fiendish ploy.'
Aloud he said: 'Chacha, why d'you want only me?
It doesn't make sense, I don't understand this decree.
Why should I remain here while the others go on?
Is there something I don't know, some hidden reason?'

Dhona burst out laughing: 'What's put that in your head?
You had better be careful and watch how you tread.
You're too green to talk back in a manner so bold;
you should heed your orders and do as you are told.'

The six ships left and were soon no longer visible,
while the seventh remained, moored by the jungle.
'Chachaji,' said Dukhey, 'what are we waiting for?
Shouldn't we leave before the tide goes out any more?'

'There's no firewood,' said Dhona. 'It just struck my mind.
Let's go down, the two of us, and see what we find.'
Dukhey guessed that a trap was about to spring.
'Firewood?' he said. 'Why? We've no need for kindling.'

'Don't argue,' said Dhona, 'when you're given an order.
That's the first lesson for any good lascar.'

'Chacha!' cried Dukhey. 'You mustn't think I'm unaware,
that what's afoot here is not a simple affair.
Those riches you got, how did they materialize?
Your cargo of beeswax is a fabulous prize.
But behind it all there's something inhuman,
it seems some force has awoken your inner demon.

Is it my life that's to be the price of your wealth?
        Are you sending me off to be waylaid in stealth?
Will you wash your hands of it before my mother?
        What'll you say to her, if I'm killed by a tiger?
When you first came to our home, what a tale you spun:
        How will my mother live, without her only son?
Your solemn promise are you now going to dishonour,
        by sending me ashore to meet my killer?'

Said Dhona: 'What nonsense is this? Have you lost your mind?
        We'd better start or we'll be left far behind.
If we don't get going, we'll be here all day;
        you go in that direction, I'll walk the other way.'

Heart in mouth, Dukhey stepped into the dark jungle,
        while Dhona watched from the shelter of a peepul.
Once the dense greenery had swallowed the boy,
        Dhona smirked, gratified by the success of his ploy.
To Dokkhin Rai he said: 'Lord, I've kept our bargain,
        I've delivered to you a tender young human.'

On the far bank

Its amber eyes glittered

Dukhey caught sight of the beast

as it watched its feast

Stepping into his ship, Dhona unloosed the rope;
watching from afar, Dukhey now gave up all hope.
'It's just as I'd thought, uncle's left me and set sail.
Death awaits me now, that'll be the end of this tale.'

Dokkhin Rai, exultant, feasted his eyes on Dukhey.
'The Rich One's kept his word, he's left me my prey.'

His maw began to tingle as he watched his prize;
in an instant he assumed his tiger disguise.
'How long has it been since human flesh came my way?
What bliss to find a victim like this sad Dukhey.'

On the far mudbank Dukhey caught sight of the beast.
Its amber eyes glittered, as it watched its feast;
with its nose a-twitch, it sniffed the spoor of its game;
its ochre stripes shimmered, like tongues of burning flame.

'That's no mere tiger,' thought Dukhey, panic-stricken;
'it's Dhona's master, come to collect his portion.'

Then at last, his mother's words rang in his head:
Use the meter of wonder, call Bon Bibi, she'd said.
But how to find the words, in this state of panic,
with the beast about to spring, grim and satanic?

It was the meter itself that came to his rescue,
like magic it summoned lines of the right hue:
'Save me, Ma Bon Bibi, before I'm torn apart;
an unearthly tiger wants to rip out my heart.
It's not a mere animal, it's a demonic being;
no earthly creature could be so conniving.
Come, I beseech you, take pity on Dukhey,
don't let this prayer be the last I ever say.'

The bounded syllables gave wings to his prayer,
to Bon Bibi it went, arrowing through the air.
'What's this I hear?' she said, turning to her brother.
'A fevered cry from a soul about to suffer.
That ever-hungry shadow-stalker must be at large,
hunting some poor soul who is lost in his raj.

His appetites grow strong when humans stoke his greed;
to show him his limits we must stop this misdeed.'

Through the tideland they streaked, moving like lightning;
they were at Dukhey's side before the tiger could spring.
Raising her voice, Bon Bibi said to her brother:
'We must teach a lesson to this artificer.
Words will not serve with him, he needs a show of force;
it'll take the strength of your arm to teach him remorse.'

'So it shall be, dear sister,' Shah Jongoli said;
like a hammer went his fist, straight to the beast's head.
The tiger reeled, so great was the force of the blow;
it jogged his memory of what'd happened before;
of how he'd lain then, clasped, corralled and canting.
Spinning around, into the forest he went streaking.

'Where will he run?' said Bon Bibi, arms akimbo,
'Brother: he must pay the price of his bravado.

He wanted to kill this innocent, this poor Dukhey;
bring him back to me and I will make him pay.'

Shah Jongoli obeyed, leaping to give chase;
many long days would pass before the end of the race.
In that time great good fortune came to Dukhey;
to Bon Bibi's own home he was spirited away.
With her love and care, he began to recover;
Each day deepening his reverence for his saviour.

Soon enough Shah Jongoli tracked down his quarry,
and dragged him back to surrender to Bon Bibi.
Dokkhin Rai, repentant, lay prostrate before her;
swearing he'd be her loyal servant forever.

After much pleading, he was at last forgiven;
never again, said she, could he hunt a human.
If he should happen to yield to temptation;
'It's you who'll be hunted. Make sure your word's not broken.

You must stay within your bounds and never transgress;
with what you have you must make do, don't seek excess.
Your first step is to find a proper way to speak,
it's come time for you to learn some better technique.
Count your syllables, it'll help rein your appetites in,
the yoke of meter will give you discipline.
It's the chaos in your mind that unbridles your desires,
by measuring your thoughts you'll learn to quench
those fires.'

This strange punishment wasn't easy for Dokkhin Rai,
        but one day he was glad he'd learnt to metrify.
''Thanks to you, Bon Bibi,' he said, falling before her,
        'I've learnt restraint, with the magic of meter.
With word-count and rhyme, I will master my needs,
        my desires I shall check, and repent for my misdeeds.'

'Good,' she said, 'but you still owe a debt to Dukhey,
        you tried to harm him, and for that you need to pay.
You must make him rich, even richer than Dhona;
        your wealth you must share, you must make him a raja.'

'So be it!' said Dokkhin Rai. 'I'll shower him with lakhs;
        you have my assurance, he'll have riches in stacks.'

So was Dukhey accepted as a brother,
        by his old nemesis, the still-unseen shape-shifter,
who gave him an embrace, though not of the body,
        but with lines lit with the magic of prosody.

VII

When Dhona and his ships returned to their port;
nary a soul noticed that the fleet was one man short.
Mona, for one, greeted him with jubilation;
He threw him a feast, a hero's celebration.
Soon word of Dhona's wealth spread all over the land;
many were those who bowed before his lordly hand.

It took a good while before Dukhey's poor mother
heard that Dhona was back, bearing a vast treasure.
Old and infirm though she was, she set off at once;
on reaching Dhona's house she knelt at the entrance.
'Tell me, Dhona,' she wailed, 'where is my loving son?
You and your men are all home, except only one.
I've long been waiting to see his face at my door.
Why isn't he home? You were with him, you know, I'm sure.'

Now at last, Dhona found the breath to answer her;
'Bhabhiji, what can I tell you? It's all a blur.
Dukhey went to the jungle, to fetch some firewood.
He didn't come back. I waited as long as I could.
I called his name, and shouted, and looked everywhere.
I think he must have strayed into a tiger's lair.
What can you do if there's a tiger in your fate?
If it's in your kismet, then it's always too late.'

The old lady shrieked, and her tears began to flow.
'What's this, Dhona? D'you want me to die of sorrow?
Dukhey was all I had, the boy was my lodestar.
You say a tiger killed him? How cruel you are!
I don't understand, how you could've let this happen.
You swore you'd bring him back; your promise you've broken.'

A crowd had gathered, drawn by her anguished lament;
their scornful eyes caused Dhona much embarrassment.

'Enough!' he said to her. 'You must stop this weeping.
I'll provide for your needs, you won't lack for a thing.
I'll send you fine foods, and sarees of rich muslin.
But this scene must end now, that's my one condition.'

The old lady cried out, as though struck by a leash.
'Dhona, d'you think I can be bought off with baksheesh?
D'you think it'll please me to gorge on sugar and ghee?
Or that I'll be consoled by fine alliballie?
Even a river of the richest dosootie,
would not be enough to serve as my dastoorie.
The fire of my grief could burn a sea of damask;
sorrow is all I have left, my body's a husk.
My son and I were poor but content with our station;
it was you, Dhona, who showed him temptation.
I'd gladly have him back, and live in poverty;
we're not you, Dhona, our needs are not nawabi.'

'Enough!' he said to her. 'You must stop this weeping.
I'll provide for your needs, you won't lack for a thing!'

Rending her hair, she cried out: 'Oh my poor son!
    Did you forget what I said, my last admonition?
I told you: in danger call on Bon Bibi;
    the Lady of the Forest will surely hear your plea.
What was it that failed you? The meter or the rhyme?
    Did your prayer lack wings? Or did your words fail to chime?'

Couched as they were, her laments could not but fly,
    they went straight to Bon Bibi, shooting across the sky.

'Dukhey,' she said, 'your mother is dying of sorrow;
    Dhona told her you're dead; it was a deathly blow.
She won't eat or drink, I fear she may not survive;
    you must go back to her if she's to stay alive.
I'll send you home mounted on my own crocodile;
    your goods will follow behind, you'll go back in style.
You'll ride the rivers, with the pomp of a raja;
    with Dokkhin Rai's wealth, you'll soon have your
    own durbar.

One final thing: with Dhona you must reconcile;
I know you must hate him, and it's true that he's vile.
But you must forgive him, rascal though he is;
to hate forever is to fall into an abyss.
And after all, it was he who brought you to me;
if not for him you would not have found Bon Bibi.
With your forgiveness, he could search for redemption;
give him one last chance, please, despite all that he's done.'

To forget his anger wasn't easy for Dukhey;
but he bowed in deference: 'I'll do as you say.
I'm your servant, as you ordain so shall it be.
Your word's law for this follower, O Bon Bibi.'

Bon Bibi called her pets, and in a short while,
Dukhey was seated royally, on a crocodile.
Behind it came others, carrying all his goods;
in a long caravan they went, through the tangled woods.

Then ashore he leapt, with a cry bursting from his throat
For there right ahead, was a shape fallen aground;

Reaching home, he kneeled, to thank his living boat;
then ashore he leapt, with a cry bursting from his throat.
For there right ahead, was a shape fallen aground;
it was still and unmoving, like a lifeless mound.
At first glance it seemed that the worst may have happened;
sorrow had brought his dear mother's life to an end.
Falling to his knees, he spluttered into her ear,
begging her to rise: 'Ma, it's me, I'm back, I'm here!'
And still she lay there unmoving, not a limb stirred;
he shook her and pleaded but his voice went unheard.

Suddenly he recalled how to make words alchemic,
it was she who'd taught him that bit of magic.
'It's true what you said about dwipodi-poyar
it saved me from becoming the tiger's shikar.
I called out to Bon Bibi, in utmost despair,
and so was I rescued, she heeded my prayer.'

The beat of the blessed meter stirred his mother;
        her eyes fluttered, and he threw his arms around her.
'Is that you, my son? Am I looking at your face?
        Has my sweet Dukhey come home, by Bon Bibi's grace?'

'Yes, I'm home, Ma,' he said. 'No longer must you grieve;
        Bon Bibi's mercy has granted me a reprieve.
Truly is her mercy beyond all measure;
        she's sent me home with great riches, an immense treasure.'

'My boy,' she said, 'you know I have no use for wealth;
        I'm happy so long you're with me, and in good health.'

Soon things came to pass as Bon Bibi had said;
        Dukhey forgave Dhona, who arranged for him to wed.
With Bon Bibi's blessings, Dukhey was no longer sad;
        he lived life in contentment, not downcast but glad,

grateful forever to his teacher, Bon Bibi;
 who'd taught him the secret of how to be happy:
All you need do, is be content with what you've got;
 to be always craving more, is a demon's lot.
A world of endless appetite is a world possessed,
 is what your munshi's learned, by way of this quest.

Dukkhey was seated royally on a crocodile

Behind it came others, carrying all his goods

Afterword

Jungle Nama is an adaptation of a legend from the Sundarban, the world's largest mangrove forest. For the people who live in and around the forest, the story of Bon Bibi is a charter that regulates every aspect of life; the beliefs associated with it dictate how they relate to the forest, and to the beings that inhabit it, especially tigers.[i]

In the villages of the Sundarban the legend is regularly enacted as a stage-play by travelling jatra companies. These enactments usually foreground the story of Dhona, Dukhey and Dokkhin Rai. I too have chosen to limit my adaptation to this episode, which forms the imaginative and dramatic core of the legend. In print versions of the legend, however, this episode accounts for only about a third of the narrative, the rest being devoted to Bon Bibi and Shah Jongoli's origins, birth and other exploits.

The two best known print versions of the legend are both entitled *Bon Bibi Johuranama* ('The Narrative of Bon Bibi's Glory'). One was composed by Munshi Mohammad Khatir, and the other by Abdur Rahim Sahib; they are both in Bengali, and both are thought to have been written in the late nineteenth century.

Both *Johuranamas* are epic poems, composed mainly in a Bengali verse meter known as dwipodi-poyar, the 'two-footed line'. This meter, which consists of rhyming couplets, has a long history and has been in wide use for centuries, in Bengali folk literature, and in such classics as the sixteenth century Bengali Mahabharat composed by the poet Kasiram Das.Verses written in this meter are meant to be chanted, sung and read aloud.[ii]

In my adaptation of the poyar meter, each line has, on average, twelve syllables, and each couplet has twenty-four. Every line also has a natural break or caesura.

My novel *The Hungry Tide* is set in the Sundarban. The Bon Bibi legend enters and informs the novel in many different ways: in the chapter entitled 'Memory', for instance, I wrote about some of the story's contexts and background. I also experimented with the poyar meter to suggest the rhythms of Bengali speech.

The story of *Jungle Nama* is told entirely in a poyar-like meter of twenty-four syllable couplets. But other than that, this is a free adaptation which does not adhere closely to printed versions of the legend. *Jungle Nama* is not intended to be a definitive version of the narrative; it is, rather, yet another re-telling of a story that already exists in many iterations.

The vocabulary of the *Bon Bibi Johuranamas* is extraordinarily hybrid, being heavily influenced by Persian and Quranic Arabic. The texts include many words that would not be familiar to speakers of standard Bengali. In *Jungle Nama,* similarly, there are words that may appear to be foreign to the English language. Yet the truth is that almost all of them, with very few exceptions, are listed in the extended Oxford English Dictionary: in that sense at least, they must be considered a part of the English lexicon. The English word 'jungle' for example, is derived from a Sanskrit root, while 'nama', as used in the titles of verse epics, comes from Persian, and means 'narrative'—or, to use an older word, 'relation'. Some of the words that figure in *Jungle Nama* are listed also in *The Ibis Chrestomathy,* which is posted on my website: http://amitavghosh.com/chrestomathy.html.

The Bon Bibi legend is a marvel of hybridity, combining Islamic, Hindu and folk elements with such fluency that it is impossible to place the story squarely in a single faith tradition. Nor is it necessary to do so, for the central tenets of the narrative—the ideas of limiting greed, and of preserving a balance between the needs of humans and those of other beings—do not belong to any one tradition: they recur frequently in the stories of forest peoples around the world. These are essential values for this era of planetary crisis, and it is on them that this adaptation rests.

The planetary crisis has upturned a vast range of accustomed beliefs and expectations, among them many that pertain to literature and literary forms. In the Before Times, stories like this one would have been considered child-like, and thus fare for children. But today, it is increasingly clear that such stories are founded on a better understanding of the human predicament than many narratives that are considered serious and adult.

Stories with images were also considered children's fare in the Before Times. This too was characteristic of an era of derangement in which humans had become so enclosed within their word-bound existence that iconography was thought to detract from the weight and seriousness of printed books. With *Jungle Nama* I knew from the start that I wanted to collaborate with an artist, in order to create a book which, rather than being 'illustrated', with images subordinated to words, would be 'illuminated', as was the case with many of the most beautiful pre-modern books, such as the magnificent miniature-studded manuscripts of the Indian subcontinent and Iran. I thought of collaborating with Salman Toor very early on: I had first seen his work at a student exhibition at the Pratt Institute, in Brooklyn, in 2009, and it was evident even then that he was prodigiously gifted. In the years since his star has risen like a meteor in the art world: so much so that I was initially hesitant to approach him, knowing that he had a major one-man show coming up at the Whitney Museum in New York in 2020.

But then the Covid 19 pandemic intervened and Salman's show was postponed, which created an opening for this project. Salman began to work on it in earnest in early September 2020. This being a time of enormous anxiety and upheaval in America, I imagined it would take him a while to get started. But what followed was an astonishing four-week-long burst of inspiration, in which images of luminous intensity would turn up on my screen several times a week. At times I felt that Salman had entered the minds of the characters, as, for instance, when he brought to life Dhona's dreams of riches, in the form of timber, honey and wax. Suffice it to say that Salman's work surpassed all my expectations: his images are precisely illuminations in the sense that they throw their own light upon the text.

That *Jungle Nama* has found this final form is due in large part to the support of Udayan Mitra, my editor at HarperCollins India, and to Bonita Shimray, the art director, who created a design that allowed text and image to shine upon each other, just as I had hoped. This book is deeply indebted to both of them.

A final and very special word of thanks is due to Leela Gandhi for her exquisitely nuanced reading of the manuscript.

Amitav Ghosh
26 October 2020

---

[i] For more on this subject the reader is referred to Annu Jalais's authoritative *Forest of Tigers: People, Politics and Environment in the Sundarbans*, Routledge 2010; and Sufia Uddin's 'Religion, Nature, and Life in the Sundarbans', *Asian Ethnology*, vol. 78, no. 2, 2019, p. 289+. Accessed 10 November 2020.

[ii] Readers interested in the history and prosodic technicalities of this meter are referred to Thibaut d'Hubert's superb study, *In the Shade of the Golden Palace: Âlâol and Middle Bengali Poetics in Arakan*, Oxford University Press, 2018. The formal features of the meter are defined in Appendix II, p. 314.

Amitav Ghosh was born in Calcutta, and grew up in India, Bangladesh and Sri Lanka; he studied in Delhi, Oxford and Alexandria. He is the author of several acclaimed works of fiction and non-fiction including *The Shadow Lines, The Glass Palace, The Hungry Tide,* the Ibis Trilogy (comprising the novels *Sea of Poppies, River of Smoke* and *Flood of Fire*), *The Great Derangement, Gun Island, The Nutmeg's Curse, The Living Mountain* and *Smoke and Ashes.*

Amitav Ghosh's work has been translated into more than thirty languages. He has been awarded and felicitated across the world. In 2019, *Foreign Policy* magazine named him one of the most important global thinkers of the past decade. The same year, the Jnanpith Award, India's highest literary honour, was conferred on him: he was the first English-language writer to receive it. In 2024, he was awarded the prestigious Erasmus Prize for his writings on the planetary crisis and climate change.

Salman Toor was born in 1983 in Lahore; he lives and works in New York. He received his MFA from Pratt Institute in Brooklyn, NY. *Salman Toor: How Will I Know*, the artist's first institutional solo exhibition, opened at the Whitney Museum of American Art, New York in 2020. Toor's work has been featured in numerous group exhibitions and projects, including *Duro Olowu: Seeing Chicago*, Museum of Contemporary Art, Chicago; *Are You Here?*, the Lahore Biennale 2018; and the 2016 Kochi-Muziris Biennale, India. Toor is the recipient of a Joan Mitchell Foundation Grant, and his work is in the permanent collections of the Museum of Contemporary Art, Chicago; the Tate, London; M Woods, Beijing; and the Whitney Museum of American Art, New York.